Conte

Jules *Rosa*

CHAPTER 1

Skateboarder in Training

Jules is playing a game on her PlayStation when her best friend Rosa comes over.

Rosa "Hi!"

Jules "Hiya."

Jules is concentrating on the game and doesn't take her eyes off the screen. Rosa looks over Jules's shoulder.

Rosa "Cool! Tony Hawk Pro Skater. That's my favourite."

Jules "Really? I thought it was Singstar. Hey, I didn't hear your Mum's car in the driveway."

Rosa “Mum didn’t bring me. I skateboarded here on my new deck.”

Jules “Deck?”

Rosa “Yes dude, deck! You mean you don’t know what a deck is and you’re playing a skateboard game?”

Jules “I know what a deck is Rosa, and why are you calling me ‘dude’?”

Rosa “So what is it?”

Jules “It’s a … er, it’s a …”

Jules glances over at Rosa.

Jules “Wow! What are you wearing?”

Rosa is dressed in a sweatshirt with a hood, baggy trousers, kneepads and a baseball cap turned backwards.

Rosa "Cool, don't you think?"

Jules "Well, kind of. When did you become an instant Tony Hawk?"

Rosa "Yesterday, when I bought my new deck at a car-boot sale."

Rosa holds up her skateboard.

Jules "But I didn't think you could skateboard?"

Rosa “I’ve been practising all day and I’m getting really rad.”

Jules “Rad? You mean ‘mad’. I’ve never seen you like this before. You on a skateboard? That’s weird.”

Rosa “It’s the new me. I’ll show you some of the tricks I’m learning.”

Jules “OK, cool.”

CHAPTER 2

Trick Chicks

Outside Jules's house, Rosa puts on her helmet and attempts to do some tricks on her skateboard.

Jules "Show me what you can do."
Rosa "OK. Here goes."

Rosa stands on her skateboard and wobbles on the spot.

Rosa “I’m just getting my balance. OK, I’m ready now. Here goes.”

Rosa slowly edges forward and uses her arms for balance.

Rosa (under her breath) “Yes! I did it without falling off. Excellent!”

Jules (laughing) "That's it? Come on, do something tricky."

Rosa "OK, OK. Don't pressure me."

Jules "I thought you'd become this amazing skater chick."

Rosa "Well, I haven't worked out all the moves yet."

Jules "Mmm, true ... not bad for only a day though."

Rosa picks up her skateboard and walks over to the driveway. Jules follows her.

Jules "Come on, try another move from Tony Hawk Pro Skater."

Rosa "Yes, OK. How's this turn?"

Jules "Hey, not bad. You look pretty cool in your skateboard clothes, like someone who could do some really amazing tricks."

Rosa "Do you think so?"

Jules "Yes, you look brilliant."

Rosa "Thanks! OK, now I'll try something else."

Jules watches as Rosa pushes herself along on the skateboard, doing a little flip as she finishes.

Jules "You're looking good. Now the moves are starting to match the look."

Rosa "I can't believe how cool this is. It feels fantastic!"

Jules "Yes, Rosa, you're looking like a professional."

Rosa "Thanks. Do you want a go?"

Jules "What, me, on the skateboard?"

Rosa "Yes."

Jules "Mmm … well, OK."

Rosa takes off her pads and helmet and hands them to Jules. Jules puts on the safety gear, then holds on to Rosa and steps on to the skateboard.

Rosa "Are you ready to go?"
Jules "OK. I'm ready."

Rosa lets go of Jules and pushes her gently forwards.

Jules "Wow! This is great."

Suddenly, the skateboard picks up speed, getting faster and faster as it heads down the pavement.

Jules "Arrrghh! How do I stop it? Rosa!"

Rosa "I'm not really sure. Just keep your arms out for balance."

Within seconds, Jules is flying down the pavement on Rosa's skateboard. Rosa chases after her.

Jules "Heeeelpp Rosaaaa!"
Rosa "Hold on Jules, hold on!"
Jules "I can't stoooppp!"
Rosa "You're doing fine. Just keep your balance!"

CHAPTER 3

World Champion Dreamer

Suddenly, a cat darts out in front of Jules. She swerves to miss it and falls onto the grass verge.

Rosa (puffing) "You OK?"
Jules "Yes, that was rad."
Rosa "Really?"

Jules "Yes, that was wicked, dude."

Rosa "Now who's talking like a professional skateboarder?"

Jules "Do you really think I'm that good?"

Rosa "Well, maybe not quite a professional, but you were really going fast!"

Jules "But did I look really brilliant?"

Rosa "You looked more scared than brilliant. The same way you looked when you found that big spider in your sleeping bag on the school trip."

The girls laugh. Then Jules gets up off the grass and steadies herself on the skateboard again.

Jules "I'm a real natural at this. I can just feel it. Maybe I should try going down ramps or something."

Rosa "I think you've bumped your head too hard. Give me a go."

Jules "Hang on, I'm not finish yet."

Rosa "But it's my skateboard."

Jules "I know, but I'm getting really good at this."

Rosa "Maybe, but it's my turn now. I want to keep practising, too."

Jules "Please, Rosa, this could be what I was born to do. I could be a future world champion and do TV adverts and things, and people will take my photo everywhere I go. And they'll say, 'There goes that really cool skater chick!' Can't you just see it?"

Rosa "In your dreams!"

Jules "And you can be my manager."

Rosa "Now you really have gone soft in the head!"

Jules "I'm serious. We could make a great team. How about it?"

Rosa "Mmm, I suppose so. Managers make loads of money. It could be fun. If you really are serious, perhaps you should try the skate park—where serious skateboarders go."

Jules “Where?”

Rosa “The skate park at the end of the street. It’s the coolest place around. If you can do it there, you can do it anywhere!”

Jules “OK! Rad dude! Let’s go!”

CHAPTER 4

Skate Park Showdown

The girls head off for the skate park.

Jules "Wow, there it is! I can see the ramp."

Rosa "Look at this place. There are so many cool skateboarders."

Jules "Look at that boy go!

The girls watch the skateboarders doing tricks on the ramp.

Rosa “That is so cool! Look at that boy kick flip.”

Jules “Yes, just like Tony Hawk.”

Rosa “So, what are you waiting for, skater chick?”

Jules "Oh, er ... well ..."

Rosa "Come on Jules!"

Jules "Look, it's your skateboard. Perhaps you should go first."

The girls notice a group of boys laughing at them and showing off. The boys start teasing Rosa and Jules, saying they wouldn't know how to skateboard.

Rosa "Hey! My friend here could easily beat you lot any day of the week."

Jules "What? Rosa! No way."

Rosa "Jules, you said I could be your manager, so listen to me. Go out there and show them what you can do."

CHAPTER 5

Go Rosa!

Rosa fixes her eyes on Jules and tries to persuade her again.

Rosa "Come on Jules, you have to do it. Or they'll think we're just scaredy-cats."

Jules "We are! Meow! Meow!"

Rosa "But you were just saying how you were born to skateboard."

Jules "Well, I've changed my mind. Call it beginner's nerves."

Rosa "Then give me the stuff and *I'll* do it."

Jules hands the safety gear and the skateboard to Rosa.

Jules "OK, here you go. But I don't fancy our chances ..."

Before Jules can finish her sentence, Rosa puts on the safety gear, takes a run up and jumps on her board.

Rosa "OK Jules, wish me luck. There's no way those guys are going to beat us!"

Jules "Way to go, Rosa. You can do it!"

Rosa "Here goes nothing!"

Rosa flies down the ramp, flipping and twisting at the top of each side as she turns.

Jules (to herself) "Wow, Rosa's brilliant at this. She's really flying!"

Jules and the boys all clap and cheer Rosa on. A few moments later, Rosa completes her routine.

Jules "Wow, Rosa, you *are* totally rad! That practice has really paid off. You were unbelievable!"

Rosa "Thanks. I even amazed myself."

Jules "No, I mean you were ..."

Rosa "Rad, wicked, brilliant, just plain excellent?"

Jules "Yes."

Rosa "Thanks, Jules."

Jules "Forget me. I think *I* should be your manager and *you* be the future world champion, skater chick!"

Rosa "It's a deal!"

GIRLS ROCK! Skateboard Lingo

carving When a skateboarder leans into the direction of their turn with their body weight, not what someone does to cut up their piece of steak!

deck A cool word for "skateboard".

kick flip When you flick your skateboard with your foot to make it spin underneath you while you are in the air.

rad To say something is rad means that it's cool. Rad is short for "radical".

skate park A park for skateboarders to try out their tricks.

Tony Hawk A skateboarding legend. He even has a PlayStation game named after him!

Skateboard Must-dos

☆ Remember to wear all the correct skateboard safety gear—grazed hands or knees, or a cracked head isn't a good look.

☆ Practise saying "dude" or "rad" often when you're trying out some new moves on a "deck".

☆ Try to always go skateboarding with a friend, because who else can you show off your tricks to?

☆ Find the nearest skate parks in your area and get someone to take you (and your friend) there. Watch the local skateboarding talent—you'll learn a lot about skateboarding by just watching others.

☆ Always try to look the part. It might not help you skateboard better but at least you'll look like you know what you're doing.

☆ If your friend doesn't have a skateboard of her own then share yours with her—that's what friends are for.

☆ On rainy days when you can't skateboard, get some paper and pencils and design your own skateboard.

Skateboard Instant Info

- The world's biggest skateboard is 4.5 metres long and can hold four people at a time.
- Skateboarding is currently the sixth most popular sport in the United States.
- Alan Ollie Gelfand invented the "Ollie". The ollie is a skateboarding trick where you leap into the air with the skateboard, keeping your feet on the board all the time.
- Some of the best female skateboarders in the world are Jaime Reyes, Vanessa Torres and Monica Shaw.

In the late 1950s, surfers in California, USA, came up with a surfing alternative when they couldn't go out in the waves. They nailed the bases of roller skates to the front and back ends of wooden planks and went "sidewalk surfing".

Two popular skate parks in the UK are Pioneer Skate Park in St Albans and The Works Skate Park in Leeds.

A major skateboarding competition for skater chicks is the All Girl Skate Jam. Contests are held all over the world including the UK. You can visit their website at www.allgirlskatejam.com.

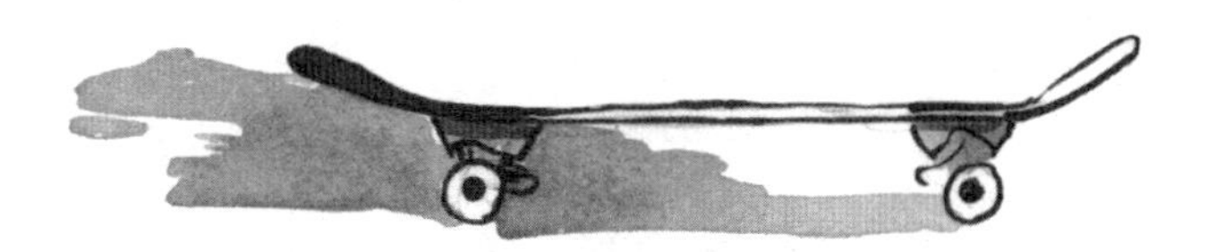

Think Tank

1. Name two pieces of safety gear you should wear to go skateboarding.
2. What else can you carve apart from meat?
3. Who is one of the greatest skateboarding legends?
4. Where does the name "Ollie" come from?
5. A kick flip is a type of milk shake. True or false?
6. If you were a skater chick, what world competition could you enter?
7. Who came up with the idea of "sidewalk surfing" in the 1950s?
8. Where's the best place to get really good at skateboarding?

Answers

1 You should wear knee pads and a helmet to go skateboarding.

2 You can carve a turn when you are on your skateboard.

3 Tony Hawk is one of the greatest skateboarding legends.

4 The ollie is named after Alan Ollie Gelfand, the man who invented it.

5 False. A kick flip is a move similar to an ollie.

6 Skater chicks should enter the All Girl Skate Jam.

7 Surfers in California came up with the idea of "sidewalk surfing" when they couldn't go in the sea.

8 A skate park is the best (and safest) place to get really good at skateboarding.

How did you score?

- If you got all 8 answers correct, then you have all the makings of a professional skater chick.

- If you got 6 answers correct, then you probably think it's totally "rad' to watch professional skaters at a skate park.

- If you got fewer than 4 answers correct, maybe skateboarding isn't your thing—but you'd still look good in the clothes.

Hey Girls!

I hope that you have as much fun reading my story as I have had writing it. I loved reading and writing stories when I was young.

Here are some suggestions that might help you enjoy reading even more than you do now.

At school, why don't you use "Skater Chicks" as a play and you and your friends can be the actors? Get a skateboard and some cool clothes like caps, hooded sweatshirts and baggy trousers, to use as props. So ... have you decided who is going to be Rosa and who is going to be Jules? And what about the narrator?

Now act out the story in front of your friends. I'm sure you'll have a great time!

You also might like to take this story home and get someone in your family to read it with you. Maybe they can take on a part in the story.

Whatever you choose to do, remember, reading and writing is a whole lot of fun!

And remember, Girls Rock!

Jacqueline Arena

Jacqueline talked to Shey, another *Girls Rock!* author.

Jacqueline "Were you good at skateboarding when you were younger?"

Shey "I was one of the best in the world."

Jacqueline "Really? What made you so good?"

Shey "I could go faster on my skateboard than anyone else."

Jacqueline "How fast was that?"

Shey "Eighty miles per hour!"

Jacqueline "No way! That's impossible."

Shey "Not when you sit on your skateboard in the back seat of your dad's car and he's driving on the motorway!"

GIRLS ROCK!

What a Laugh!

Q What is the hardest thing about riding a skateboard?

A The road!

GIRLS ROCK!

The Sleepover

Pool Pals

Bowling Buddies

Girl Pirates

Netball Showdown

School Play Stars

Diary Disaster

Horsing Around

Newspaper Scoop

Snowball Attack

Dog on the Loose

Escalator Escapade

Cooking Catastrophe

Talent Quest

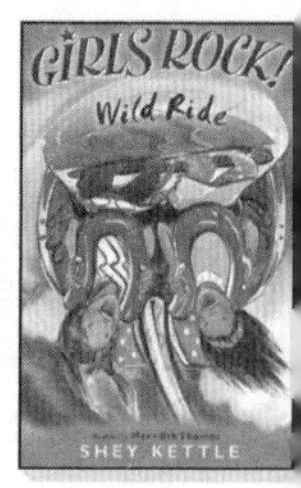

Wild Ride

Camping Chaos

Mummy Mania

Skater Chicks